The Berenstain Bears
DOLLAR$
AND
ENE

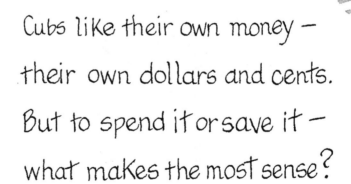

Cubs like their own money —
their own dollars and cents.
But to spend it or save it —
what makes the most sense?

A First Time Book®

The Berenstain Bears
DOLLAR$
AND
ENE

Stan & Jan Berenstain

Random House 🏠 New York

Copyright © 2001 by Berenstain Enterprises, Inc. All rights reserved under International and
Pan-American Copyright Conventions. Published in the United States by Random House, Inc.,
New York, and simultaneously in Canada by Random House of Canada Limited, Toronto.
www.randomhouse.com/kids www.berenstainbears.com
Library of Congress Cataloging-in-Publication Data: Berenstain, Stan, 1923– The Berenstain Bears
dollars & sense / Stan & Jan Berenstain. p. cm. — (A first time book) SUMMARY: Mama and Papa Bear
   try to teach Brother and Sister the value of money and how to manage their allowance.
   ISBN 0-375-81124-9 (trade) — ISBN 0-375-91124-3 (lib. bdg.)
   [1. Finance, Personal—Fiction. 2. Bears—Fiction.]
   I. Title: Berenstain Bears dollars and sense. II. Berenstain, Jan, 1923– . III. Title.
   PZ7.B4483 Bemke 2001 [E]—dc21 00-041475
   Printed in the United States of America January 2001 10 9
   RANDOM HOUSE and colophon are registered trademarks of Random House, Inc.

Money wasn't a big problem in the Bear family's tree house down a sunny dirt road deep in Bear Country. But it *was* a problem—at least where cubs Brother and Sister were concerned. They knew some things about money. They knew that Papa wasn't made of it, that it didn't grow on trees, and that they should save it for a rainy day. Papa had told them those things many times. What they didn't know about money was how to manage it.

The cubs liked money. They had liked it even before they knew you could buy things with it. They liked coins better than paper money because you could do things with coins.

They liked to roll them.

They liked to spin them.

They liked to stack them.

As they got a little older, they liked to play "heads or tails" with them.

But by keeping their eyes and ears open at the supermarket, the hardware store, and the clothing store, they soon learned that you could do a lot more with money than just play with it. You could *buy* things with it.

You could buy all sorts of things.

Ice cream from the Good Humor Be[ar]

rides on the Bucking Duck at the mall,

balloons from the
balloon bear at the park.

As time went on, the cubs learned more about money. They learned the difference between the dollar sign, which was an "S" with two lines through it, and the cent sign, which was a "C" with one line through it.

"Baseball cards? Wedding dress?" shouted Papa. "You must think I'm made of money. You must think money grows on trees!" The cubs backed away. All they wanted was some green money. All they got was Papa red in the face.

Mama had been watching. She knew it was time to calm things down, and she had an idea how to do it.

"If you cubs will excuse us," she said, "there are some things I'd like to discuss with your papa."

"My dear," said Mama, "it's not going to do any good to shout at the cubs. It's as much our fault as it is theirs that they don't understand about money. It's up to us to teach them how to manage money."

"But *how*?" asked Papa.

Check 001

(Your name)

(Your address)

001

DATE _____

PAY TO THE
ORDER OF _____ $ _____

_____ DOLLARS

BEAR COUNTRY BANK

FOR _____

NON-NEGOTIABLE

RECORD

DATE _____

ALLOWANCE _____

CHECK _____

ALLOWANCE
LEFT _____

Check 002

(Your name)

(Your address)

002

DATE _____

PAY TO THE
ORDER OF _____ $ _____

_____ DOLLARS

BEAR COUNTRY BANK

FOR _____

NON-NEGOTIABLE

RECORD

DATE _____

ALLOWANCE _____

CHECK _____

ALLOWANCE
LEFT _____

Check 003

(Your name)

(Your address)

003

DATE _____

PAY TO THE
ORDER OF _____ $ _____

_____ DOLLARS

BEAR COUNTRY BANK

FOR _____

NON-NEGOTIABLE

RECORD

DATE _____

ALLOWANCE _____

CHECK _____

ALLOWANCE
LEFT _____

ECORD

004

(Your name)

(Your address)

PAY TO THE
ORDER OF _____ $ _____

DATE _____

_____ DOLLARS

BEAR COUNTRY BANK

FOR _____

NON-NEGOTIABLE

NCE _____

NCE _____

004

ECORD

005

(Your name)

(Your address)

PAY TO THE
ORDER OF _____ $ _____

DATE _____

_____ DOLLARS

BEAR COUNTRY BANK

FOR _____

NON-NEGOTIABLE

ANCE _____

ANCE _____

005

ECORD

006

(Your name)

(Your address)

PAY TO THE
ORDER OF _____ $ _____

DATE _____

_____ DOLLARS

BEAR COUNTRY BANK

FOR _____

NON-NEGOTIABLE

ANCE _____

ANCE _____

006

"I suggest that we begin giving them a regular weekly allowance," she said.

"Hmm," said Papa. "That's an interesting idea. Then perhaps they will learn to be more responsible about money."

"An allowance?" said Sister.

"What's an allowance?" asked Brother.

"An allowance," said Papa, "is a sum of money that you will get at the beginning of every week. It will be up to you to manage it—to spend it or save it as you see fit."

The cubs looked at each other as if they didn't believe him. It seemed too good to be true.

"And here's your first week's allowance," said Papa.

Brother and Sister looked at the small pile of money Papa had placed in front of each of them. Then they grabbed the money and were out the front door, down the front steps, and on the road to tow faster than you can say "weekly allowance."

"Hmm," said Papa.
"Double hmm,"
said Mama.

When the cubs returned, they each had a pile of candy bars, bubble gum, and trading cards.

They had spent their whole allowance on the first day of the week.

And they did the same thing the next week,

and the next,

and the next.

It was clear to Mama and Papa that the allowance idea wasn't working as planned, and it certainly wasn't teaching the cubs how to manage money.

The cubs would quickly eat the candy bars and get tired of the other things they bought. Then they would mope and groan because they didn't have any money left for the rest of the week.

"Mama," said Brother. "I don't think this allowance idea is working out."

"I quite agree," said Mama. "But what do you suggest?"

"*A bigger allowance!*" said the cubs as one.

"Possibly," said Mama. "But that is something we'll have to discuss with your papa."

"Well, let's discuss it with him right now," said Sister.

"Oh, no," said Mama. "Papa is balancing the checkbook. I never interrupt your papa while he's balancing the checkbook."

Hmm. Checkbook, thought Mama. Our checkbook helps Papa and me manage *our* money. It gives us a chance to think about how we should spend it. It gives us a record of how much money we have spent and how much we have left.

Mama went into the kitchen. She rummaged around in the cupboard drawer. It was filled with things she wasn't quite ready to throw away. Among the things were some extra checkbooks that were left over from when she changed banks. But how to explain the idea of checks and checkbooks to the cubs, she wondered.

Mama told Papa what she had in mind. Then she explained the idea of checks to the cubs.

"Do you mean you're taking *away* our allowances?" protested Brother.

"Not at all," said Papa. "As a matter of fact, we're increasing your allowances. But instead of giving them to you at the beginning of each week so that you can go out and spend them before they burn a hole in your pockets, we're going to hold them for you. Then when you want a little pocket money or want to buy something, you write out a check.

"Here, I'll show you how it's done.

"First you make it out to 'Cash,' like so. Then you put how much it's for—in words as well as numbers so there can't be any mistake. Then you write what it's for on this line and sign it at the bottom and on the back. Then you give it to Mama and she gives you the money and keeps a record. It's that simple."

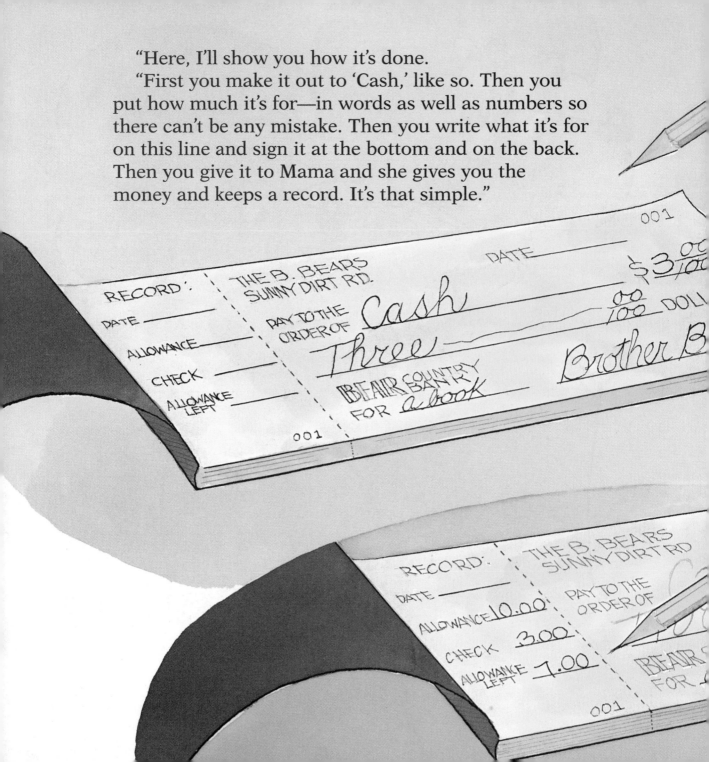

Brother got the idea right away and gave Mama the check for three dollars, and she gave him the cash. He changed his mind about spending five dollars (half his allowance) on baseball cards and bought a baseball book instead. Sister changed her mind, too. She decided to save her first week's allowance and buy the Bearbie wedding dress with her *next* week's allowance so she would still have ten dollars left.

"Now, that's what I call *money managing*," said Mama to Papa.